Boned By The T-Rex

The Dino Love Bone Series
Book II

Arrow Rivendell

Dedicated to Lana Del Rey, because she tastes like Pepsi-Cola. I know you are having trouble finding inspiration for your next album. Think Dino Erotica, baby!

1. THE GREEN COCK POCKET

Liwen Need-A-Dick lay awake, unable to sleep, listening to the distant bellowing of the t-rex on the high plateau, as the feint light of dawn emerged through the trees.

The male-only Terris tribe, two-pump chumps who had given up on women and taken to the butt-fuckery, visited the night before for their monthly mating attempt.

They did not stay long, and Liwen was passed over again. She truly lived up to her name. No dick would come near her, as her pussy was the stinkiest in her all-female tribe.

Right now, that coochie was stuffed

with sage, rosemary, thyme and mint leaves. This was her tribe's post-sex ritual, to cleanse the cock pocket, and she participated even though she got nothing. Hence the Terrisses called their tribe the Green Box Ganguros.

They called me stinky again, Liwen thought. *Everyone calls me stinky.*

She looked over at Pascale Hunts, the manliest female in her tribe, and its lead huntress.

Pascale's mouth was stuffed with the sage-mint-herbs mixture.

Due to her hairy legs, slight mustache and large head, the Terrisses seemed to like Pascale the best.

Liwen reached out to stroke Pascale's hair, but Pascale pulled back immediately.

"Stinky, I may have sucked fourteen dicks tonight, and I was prepared to suck more, if Madhu hadn't ruined it, that bitch," Pascale said, "but I'm not touching your nappy cock cave."

"Sorry. Sorry. I was sleeping," Liwen said.

"Yeah right. Stupid chickadee," Pascale said, as she rolled over, putting her back to Liwen.

"But, I-"

Then a tremendous scream pierced the silence of the valley.

The tribe sprung awake, grabbed their spears, and crouched defensively against the rocks inside the caves, waiting for the attack.

Then they heard another, louder, piercing scream. It came from the watering hole or perhaps across the valley.

Pascale stuck her head out from the caves first. She cautiously stepped out, then started down the path, toward the watering hole.

The tribe gingerly trailed behind her.

The screaming continued. The Green Box Ganguro girls passed nervous glances between each other.

Pascale, ever the huntress, focused only on the path ahead, her senses on high.

When she crest the first hill, she froze. The tribe squatted, defensive, with their spears at the ready.

Pascale giggled.

"Well, come here," she said. "You chicks got to see this."

The tribe cautiously stepped forward, but once they reached Pascale, they too saw the source of the screams.

Across the valley, in the fire-clearing, Madhu, the master cockdoll maker and Lewin's former apprentice, was getting it good and hard from a triceratops.

The three-horned face bull had pinned her, or she had figured out a way to get pinned, between the bull and his cow.

The bull drove his huge cock into Madhu, and the whole tribe now recognized the sounds of ecstasy in Madhu's screams.

She was getting boned hard by the triceratops and she liked it.

This was nothing like the sad and sorry pumping from the Terrisses, so the tribe collectively swooned, entranced.

The bull shook and grinded and Madhu wailed and moaned and coiled and tightened. Dust rose around them.

And then they both came, their orgasms shaking the very ground, and Madhu's pleasure shrieks filling the valley.

2. THE COCKDOLL TEACHER

The night before, the tribe had banished Madhu when her cockdolls had become too powerful a temptation for the Terrisses and ruined their mating ritual.

Now, the Green Box Ganguro viewed Madhu in awe.

Across the valley, the three-horned face climbed off of Mahdu and his cow. Madhu fell to the ground, immobile.

Yet the tribe could not move. They just stared across the valley, at the lifeless and spent body of Madhu.

"Is she dead," Pascale asked.

Madhu lay still, while the bull and his cow ambled into the forest.

Pascale rushed down the trail, hit the watering hole full-stride with a dive, then popped up on the opposite bank.

Liwen, Madhu's sister Nisha, and the other tribe mates followed quickly after Pascale.

When the tribe reached Madhu, she lay on her back, panting, beaming.

"Are you-," Pascale said. "Are you alive?"

Madhu opened her eyes, shocked to see her tribe mates standing there. She was covered in triceratops love juice and cow dung, but she was smiling from ear to ear.

She was more than happy. She beamed and nothing could remove the smile from her face.

She sat up, then stood herself up strong, hovering above the tribe somehow.

The tribe knelt down, bowing to her.

On bended knee, Pascale held out her spear to Madhu.

Madhu took the spear and thus became leader of the tribe.

The girls hooted and hollered and shrieked and celebrated their new leader.

They crowded around Madhu, hugging her, patting her back, undeterred by the triceratops jizz and butt nuggets which covered her.

Then Liwen tried to hug Madhu, but Madhu pushed her back.

"Not you, Stinky," Madhu said. "You cast the first stone."

Madhu pointed her spear toward the high plateau, above the Terris camp.

"You go," Madhu said.

Liwen wanted to argue, to fight with Madhu, but one look at the faces of her tribe mates told her it was no use.

"No. No," Liwen shrieked. "I taught you how to make the cockdolls. I taught you everything. I taught you."

"Go."

"I taught you everything," Liwen screamed. "I taught you. You- You- If you can bang the three-horned face. Then I can bang the tyrant lizard."

The tribe gasp.

"That's right, I will bang the t-rex. And I will bonk-bonk harder than you," Liwen said. "Then you will all bow before me and kiss my coochie, fuzzy monkeys."

"Eeeewwwww," Pascale gasped.

Liwen tightened and shook and glared at Pascale and Madhu.

"Fuzzy monkey bitches," she said.

Liwen stormed off, disappearing into the dense, green forest, while Pascale and Madhu laughed.

3. THE SISTERS

As soon as she was out of sight of her tribe, panic hit Liwen. She sprinted through the forest. She had to beat the tribe back to the caves.

At a full run, she dove into the watering hole, pulled herself out on the other side, then dashed up the trail.

She tore into camp, to her sleeping grass. She snatched the first reed basket she could find and stuffed it with mint, sage, rosemary and thyme.

Then she grabbed carrots and onions and dried eomaia meat and flung the basket over shoulder.

She grabbed an extra spear, then dug under her sleeping grass.

She pulled out a small, triceratops tail impaler and tossed it aside.

Next came a triple-entry velociraptor finger dildo, which she quickly stuffed into her bag.

Rushing, trembling, and listening for the tribe, she tossed the whole grass bed over.

"There you are," she said.

She grabbed the large, t-rex leg bone, double penetrator.

"I couldn't leave without you," she said, as she scampered out of the caves, running up the hill.

Ahead of her, she saw the silhouettes of the younger members of the tribe, who she had run off the night before, so as to not tempt the Terrisses with their flat chests and more man-like bodies.

She paused behind a tree, hiding, thinking about her next move.

"I see you, Liwen," Aikaterina said. "Now's not the time to play."

"Sister," Liwen said. "I'm-"

Liwen froze. Aikaterina's face was swollen on one side, black and bloody. Scratches of blood ran down her back and arms.

"What happened," Liwen said. "Did the Terrisses-"

"We heard the screams this morning, coming from the valley," Aikaterina said.

"We gathered in a clearing, to try to glimpse what was happening," Rose, Liwen's other sister, said as she walked up.

"Then-"

"Then it came," Rose said. "A beast t-rex, frothy and scattered. It didn't attack for food-"

"It ate no one," Aikaterina said.

"But it attacked," Rose said. "It bit and shook and stomped and held Nish-Nish and Brownie in its mouth."

"Then spit them out," Aikaterina said.

"Then- Then it roared and stomped a

few more of us," Rose said.

"It ran off," Aikaterina said.

"I have no, no-," Rose said.

"No idea," Aikaterina finished.

"No. It makes sense," Liwen said. "I'll tell you why."

Liwen sat down against the tree. Rose and Aikaterina plopped down beside her. Some of the other younger girls stumbled up, also bloody and bruised, and dropped down behind them, as Liwen spoke.

"What you heard was Madhu," Liwen said. "The screaming. The animals are turning, and Madhu figured out- She decided. Madhu got boned by the triceratops. Boned good and hard. Like a champion warrior."

Liwen let that last line sink in. The girls were listening. Some tired, some confused. Except Rose. Rose glared at Liwen.

"The t-rex that came through," Liwen said. "He wasn't looking for food. He would have eaten you. He was looking for a mate. A Ganguro mate."

The girls gasped.

"He was looking for me," Liwen said.

Some of the girls gasped. Others giggled. But Rose glared at her.

"Don't tease us, Stinky," Rose said. "We're in no mood."

Rose sprung up, rock in hand. Liwen jumped up, holding her arms up to protect herself.

"I do not tease," Liwen said. "I am going to live on the high plains, to boink with the t-rex, where I belong. Come with me. Help me."

"Liar," Rose screamed, and she threw the rock.

Liwen blocked the rock with her hand.

"No," Liwen shouted.

Aikaterina grabbed a rock and sent it toward Liwen, hitting her in the chest. Liwen fell back, rolled down the hill, the put a tree between her and the girls.

They all held rocks now.

"I do not kid," Liwen screamed. "And I ask you to join me. Madhu is the leader now. She will not have you in the camp. You must come with me."

"Liar," Rose said, and threw her rock, hitting the tree.

Then a flurry of rocks rained down on Liwen, as all the girls unleashed their anger on her. She crouched and used her arms to block what she could.

After the first wave, Liwen ran downhill, away from the caves, away from the young girls.

"Stinky, Stinky, run away," the girls chanted. "Stinky bitch."

But they did not chase after Liwen.

4. THE OFFER

Liwen ran in a circular path, going downhill first, then sideways away from the caves, and finally back uphill, toward the high plateaus where the t-rex lived.

More than hallway up, she reached a fork in the path. To the right, the trail led to the high plains. To the left, it led to the Terris camp.

Liwen paused, considering her options.

She chose the path to the Terrisses.

Slowly, she snuck up toward their caves, hiding behind trees and rocks, unsure if they had sentries posted, unsure if they would attack her.

Finally, the shadows emerged as the

sun fell below the horizon.

She quickened her pace, but stayed quiet, hanging in the shadows.

Then she saw them, circled around a bonfire, hooting and hollering.

She saw their leader, Black Kenny, first. He ass was pumping hard and fast into Chubalito's mouth.

"Sons of whores," Liwen muttered.

Chubalito sat on the front horn of Madhu's cockdoll masterpiece, the triple-rider triceratops head.

Beside him, Kowtow serviced Brown-Sniffer and Scunt took the full bore of Bootlick's cock.

Leave it to the Terrisses to turn a triple-rider into a six person suck off, Liwen thought.

Then she felt a sharp prick against her ribs.

"Stinky, what are you doing here," Jolly-Guzzler said, holding a spear on her.

"I- I- I can suck a dick too," Liwen

said.

"Walk," Jolly-Guzzler said.

Liwen stepped out from the shadows, with Jolly-Guzzler's spear urging her on.

"Black Kenny," Jolly-Guzzler shouted.

Black Kenny turned, pulling his huge erect cock out of Chubalito's mouth.

"Damn it! Damn it," he screamed.

He grabbed his cock and pumped it hard and fast.

"Damn it," he screamed.

"I can suck that cock," Liwen screamed. "I can suck a cock as good as any man."

"On your knees," Black Kenny commanded. "Hold her arms."

Liwen fell to her knees and Jolly-Guzzler held her hands behind her back.

She opened her mouth, ready, willing and excited.

"You interrupt me," Black Kenny said.

He smacked his huge cock across her face. Liwen tried to take it in, tried to suck it, but he pulled his cock back.

Then he smacked her with it again and again and again.

Each time, Liwen tried to suck it, tried to get any piece of it in her and each time Black Kenny pulled his throbbing member away from Liwen.

"Please, please. Let me suck that cock," Liwen begged, wet with anticipation.

Black Kenny pumped his cock hard twice, then grabbed Jolly-Guzzler's head and rammed it onto his member.

"No," Liwen screamed.

Black Kenny shook and twisted and tightened and howled and came.

"No. Please," Liwen screamed.

Black Kenny pumped his chest hard, then smiled at Liwen.

"I would not make you stronger with my come, Stinky," he said. "Each time I spend my juice, the taker gets stronger."

The Terrisses shrieked and howled.

"I- I- But," Liwen said. "I-"

"There's nothing here for you, Stinky," Black Kenny said.

"I-, I- Did you hear the screams this morning," Liwen said.

"Yes. Yes, we did," Black Kenny said. "Were you attacked?"

"That was Madhu," Liwen said.

"The master cockdoll maker," Black Kenny said.

"I taught her everything she knows," Liwen said. "I brought you these."

Liwen pulled out her t-rex double rider and triple-entry velociraptor fingers.

"I can live with you," Liwen said. "Make these for you."

Black Kenny picked up the t-rex bone, eyeing the work. Then he sniffed it and tossed it aside.

"The work is subpar," he said. "And it has been fouled by you."

"But-"

"Madhu's is superior," Black Kenny said. "Much, much better. And we have a full stock."

"Mahdu is the leader now," Liwen said. "Those screams were hers. She rode the three-horned face."

Smack. Liwen fell back as Black Kenny's hand flew across her face.

"Liar," Black Kenny said.

"I do not lie. I do not kid," Liwen said. "I-"

Then she froze as Black Kenny grabbed Jolly-Guzzler's spear.

"I have come to ride the t-rex with my front butt," Liwen said. "That's why I have come."

Black Kenny smiled and laughed good and hard. The rest of the Terrisses joined in the laughter chorus.

"I- I- I," Liwen said. "I- You can have

me first. But tomorrow, I ride the t-rex."

"Now this we will need to see," Black Kenny said. "For if you are lying to us, you'll be dead. But you'll not trick us either. No man here will touch your stink box."

5. THE BROWNIE

"E.S.P.," Madhu said as she awoke, smiling. "I've got the best case of E.S.P. ever."

Nish-Nish brought Madhu a bowl full of green paste, made up of mint, lemon verbena and thyme, which she spread on Madhu's cooter, as this was thought to cure E.S.P, or extra sore pussy.

Pascale was already up, sharpening spears with Rose and Nisha.

"So you're going then," Madhu asked.

"We will feast on the meat of the t-rex tonight," Pascale said.

"He attacked us," Rose said. "We must kill him."

Madhu shook her head and smiled and lay back down, resting her sore coot.

Liwen also woke with a smile, but for different reasons. She did not get the sperm from the Terrisses, as she had hoped. However, she did get a full belly of eomaia meat and a soft grass bed by a warm fire, which were far better prospects than she anticipated.

Then she remembered what she needed to do today.

The Terrisses joked and laughed, as they ate breakfast, but Liwen was silent, thinking of her day.

"It's time," Black Kenny finally said.

Liwen gathered her spears, flipped her basket full of cockdolls over her shoulder, and headed out of caves, followed by the Terris tribe.

They hiked hard, climbing up the hill toward the high plateau. They heard the mighty t-rex smashing the ground, howling and wailing, t-rex flesh pounding t-rex flesh as they sorted out pack dominance.

They crawled on all fours to the crest of the hill. The t-rex screeched loudly, drowning out any hope of talking, but when Liwen's head popped over the hill, everything stopped.

In unison, all the heads of the t-rex herd turned toward Liwen.

The pack screeched then charged. The Terrisses scattered in all directions as the t-rex pack tore into the forest, smashing trees and chomping after them.

A large green t-rex caught Kowtow in its mouth, bit him in half, then gulped down his body parts.

Liwen bolted with two males, Blackie and Brownie, hot on her trail.

She ran into the forest, but Blackie jumped in front of her, tore a tree up with his mighty jaws, and tossed it down in front of her path.

Liwen bolted to the clearing, and Brownie steered her toward the rock slab.

There, the two t-rex cornered Liwen.

She trembled with fear. She held her spear out and roared, trying to make herself larger.

The t-rex sniffed at her, then turned toward each other.

Roaring, Blackie thrashed at Brownie, knocking heads.

Brownie backed up, braced its head, then charged Blackie. He caught Blackie just below the ribs, rolled him over, then pounded his head into Blackie's rib cage.

Blackie rolled off, squawking, and stomped the ground. He squealed again at Brownie, then pooped on the ground and ran off.

Brownie turned his attention back to Liwen. He sniffed again and scrapped at the ground. He squealed.

Liwen held her spear up, protecting herself.

Brownie bit quickly onto the spear, tossing it aside.

He sniffed Liwen again and shook his tail.

Liwen dug furiously into her basket and pulled out her two-sided, t-rex leg bone cockdoll. She held up, sword-like, to protect herself.

Brownie sniffed at it, then backed off and stomped up and down, up and down.

Liwen saw it then: the enormous, erect penis of the t-rex.

Immediately she understood, he was doing his mating dance. The t-rex were fighting over her.

A wave of relief and satisfaction swept over Liwen. She relaxed and dropped the cockdoll leg bone.

She tore off her shirt, spun around the rock, and lifted up her loin cloth, giving the t-rex easy access.

Brownie shook and stomped and moved in.

Then Pascale appeared above her. She gave a t-rex howl and dove into Blackie's still smoldering butt mud pile.

She rolled in the t-rex dung, covering her body, then she jumped up and ran to Liwen.

Pascale pushed Liwen aside, then

stuck her ass in the air, waiting for Brownie.

Brownie moved in. Liwen turned, giving him easy access again.

Brownie sniffed Liwen, then sniffed Pascale. He sniffed Liwen again.

Brownie stepped toward Liwen. He crouched down, bit Liwen's hair, then tossed her aside.

Quickly, Brownie moved on top of Pascale, and just as quickly was inside her.

Pascale took that giant t-rex cock without missing a beat, as the t-rex thrust and pounded her cock pocket.

Pascale moaned in pleasure, as Brownie snorted and pumped and dug into her.

Furious, Liwen grabbed her two-sided anal intruder, and swung it at Pascale's head.

With the beast thrusting, Pascale blocked the intruder with her arm, then snatched it out of Liwen's hand.

The t-rex roared. Pascale spun around, then stuck the intruder into the beast's ass.

The r-rex squealed with pleasure, then violently thrust and thrust and thrust its hard cock into Pascale.

She panted and screamed and loved it, all the while ramming the cockdoll into the t-rex's ass.

Pascale's orgasm came quickly, rising in her toes, making her whole body shake.

"Bang harder," she screamed. "Bang harder!"

The t-rex somehow understood, and he thrust harder, violently pounding Pascale's cock pocket.

Together, filling the plateau with their pants and wails, they tightened and pushed and roared and came.

Pascale fell to the ground, spent.

Brownie stood up, shook his back, then turned toward Liwen.

He sniffed Liwen.

Excited, Liwen jumped up, pushed up her loin cloth, and stuck her ass in the air, ready for the t-rex love bone.

But Brownie just walked away.

THE END

ARROW RIVENDELL

ABOUT THE AUTHOR

Arrow Rivendell is clearly a pen name. I mean, if you wrote dinosaur po-, er, erotica, would you put your real name on it? I mean, what would they say at the "club"?

Special Preview

Boned By The Baryonyx

The Dino Love Bone Series
Book III

ARROW RIVENDELL

1. THE FIRE EYE THRUST

After the t-rex attack, Nisha Fire-Crotch and Rose Poonani crawled back, through the underbrush, toward the piercing and torturous screams of their tribe mates, which filled the valley.

They had come to seek revenge on the t-rex, to kill the one which attacked their village that very dawn.

But the t-rex herd turned on them, sniffing out the huntresses, as well as the all-male Terris tribe, who were on the other side of the mountain, hunting as well.

Nisha and Rose saw Kowtow Terris take the brunt of the attack, cut in two by the razor sharp teeth of a tyrant lizard, and then eaten while still alive.

"Douche bag," Nisha mumbled, as they watched him die, feeling nothing.

Then they heard Pascale Hunts, their lead huntress, paying a violent price for chasing the t-rex. It was her screams which filled the plateau.

It sounded like she too was getting eaten alive.

So they crawled through the underbrush, toward the screams, to send Pascale to the other side, and hopefully the t-rex as well.

In the underbrush, Nisha spotted Black Kenny and Brown-Sniffer Terris, heading the same way, and gave them a nod.

Silently, they nodded back.

"They can help take the t-rex," Nisha said.

Rose nodded.

"But we will have to share," Nisha said.

Pascale's screaming continued.

Nisha and Rose circled around the screaming, climbing above the rocks, out of sight, to attack from above.

But when Nisha poked her head over, spotting Pascale, she froze.

"You've got to eye this," she said. Then she stood up.

Rose crawled up beside her, then cautiously poked her head over the rocks.

"Butter my butt and call me a biscuit," Rose said.

Down below them, against the rock slab, a Brownie t-rex was anally intruding Pascale something fierce.

The t-rex was thrust, thrust, thrusting away and Pascale was squealing with delight.

"Bang harder! Bang harder! Bang harder," Pascale screamed. "Fill my gizz hole."

And the t-rex knew, he somehow knew, and moved as one with Pascale, humping away to her screams and wails and pleasure shrieks.

And now Nisha and Rose were jealous.

Black Kenny and Brown-Sniffer saw it too. They stood entranced, as Pascale's coot tamed the mighty tyrant lizard.

The t-rex banged, Pascale wailed and soon she quaked as the t-rex unloaded his giant cock juice into Pascale's orgasmic, shaking body.

And then it was silent.

Pascale fell down, limp. The t-rex rolled off of her.

Then Nisha spotted Liwen, beside the t-rex, covered in t-rex dung, ass in the air.

Liwen was trying to seduce the t-rex too.

The Brownie t-rex sniffed at Liwen, then picked her up by the hair and flung her aside.

The t-rex sprinted off, back toward his herd, flexing his tail.

"Wow," Nisha said to Rose. "Even the t-rex won't bonk, or chow, your stinky sister."

"Would you give that stinky coot the old in-out, in-out," Rose asked.

Nisha did not need to answer.

ARROW RIVENDELL

Made in the USA
Middletown, DE
10 November 2016